Diary of a *Farting* Ghast

*An **Unofficial** Minecraft Diary*

By,

M.T. Lott

Table of Contents

Chapter 1

My name is Todd, and I am a Minecraft ghast.

As you might have guessed, I spawned in the Nether. I like it here in the Nether. It is warm and not very bright. I spend most of my days floating around chilling.

The only other thing I do with any regularity is to emit high-pitched cat-like noises.

At least, that's what I did until everyone found out about my ... uh, well ... my problem.

You see, I don't shoot fireballs out of my mouth like a normal ghast. No, sir.

The only thing that comes out of my mouth – other than the high-pitched cat-like noises, of course – are giant clouds of gas.

And, it is not just gas from belching or some sort of awesome and mysterious Nether gas either.

It's ... well, there is no really polite way to put this ... it's fart gas.

And this just isn't any old typical fart gas, but some of the most hideous, stinkiest, funkiest fart gas anyone in the Nether has ever smelled.

In fact, there have been some very serious tragedies relating to my gassy mouth.

But, I did not know I was different from any of the other ghasts when I first spawned. Actually, when I first spawned, I didn't know anything, really.

What is really amazing is that I went from spawning, to making three friends, to discovering my hideous stench, to battling Herobrine, all in just a few days.

Through it all, I did my best to maintain my chill.

Why don't I tell you about it?

Chapter 2

It all started, as I suppose it all must, when I spawned. What had gone before my spawning, was of no concern to me.

I had spawned in mid-air, floating in the manner of all ghasts.

Very shortly thereafter, I began to drift. I had no idea where I was going or what I should do. Like most ghasts, I valued chillin' above all else.

Check out my chillin' face:

Just a few minutes later, my chill vibe was shattered when I met a strange bouncing cube. I looked at the cube and I said, "My name is Todd. What's your name?"

"My name is Joe," he said.

"Nice to meet you, Joe. I just spawned. I am chilling and exploring," I said.

The cube bounced up and down a couple of times and said, "Well, everything in the Nether looks the same. Everything is kind of purplish and orange-ish, and the air is warm and steamy because we are deep within the ground and there is lava everywhere."

"Oh," I said, slightly disappointed. "Well, are there any more creatures like me in the Nether?"

The magma cube looked at me like I had caught a case of The Stupids.

"Of course there are more creatures like you," he said. "You ghasts practically run the place. Duh."

When he said that, I became very excited.

First of all, I now knew that I was a "ghast." Secondly, if there were lots more ghasts like me, then I would be able to have lots of friends.

Of course, I could also be friends with this magma cube, maybe.

I tried to be friendly to the cube and said, "Where do you live? I'll try to stop by your house later."

"I live anywhere and everywhere. No permanent address," said Joe. "I just hop around and wait for players to appear. When they do, I attack them."

"Players? Are they creatures of the Nether as well?" I asked.

"No," said Joe bitterly. "They come from the Overworld down into the Nether to steal our resources and kill us. They are jerks."

I was very concerned about these players. I didn't really yet think of the Nether or its resources as "mine," but since I had spawned here, I did feel some attachment to it.

Anyway, I did not want people coming to where I lived and destroying it. It did not seem right. Plus, it would upset my chill vibe.

"Well Joe, thanks for the information. I'll be sure to keep a lookout for any players while I am exploring," he said.

"Yeah, goodbye or whatever," said the magma cube.

"Bye," I said.

As I was leaving, Joe asked, "Hey, um, do you smell that?"

"Smell what?" I asked. I did not smell anything.

"It smells like a fart blast," said Joe.

I shook my tentacles. "No. I don't smell anything," I said.

"Weird," said Joe. "I could have sworn it was a fart. Whatever. Later, ghast."

"Peace," I said as I floated on, exploring my new environment.

Chapter 3

As I floated around, lazily observing the Nether, I came across a group of strange creatures that I now know to be zombie pigmen.

There were four of them wandering around in a group together. Their pink, rotten flesh exuded a strange putrid odor. It was not at all pleasant, but not entirely repulsive either.

"Hello there," I called to the hoard of strange looking creatures. "What are you supposed to be?"

One of them looked over at me and said slowly, "Careful, ghast. Don't you know better than to insult a horde of zombie pigmen?"

"A fitting and descriptive name for you all," I said. "By the way, my name is Todd."

"We have names too, but we don't feel like telling them to you," said another one of the zombie pigmen.

I did not like their grumpy rudeness, but I knew that because they were pigmen, they had terrible lives to begin with. So, I did not take it personally.

I mean, *dang*, they were ugly.

I guess I should not be too upset that they were rude. I would *not* let them harsh my chill vibe.

"So, guys, do you know where I can find any other ghasts nearby to talk to?" I asked.

They all looked at me quizzically and shook their heads.

"No," said one of them. "We have been wandering around

in this same area for as long as any of us can remember. No ghasts have floated by during that period."

I was a little dismayed by their lack of initiative or ambition. What good is being spawned if you are just going wander around in the same spot for the rest of your life? I mean, I respect people who like to relax and chill, but these pigmen just seemed pathetic and useless.

"Okay, guys, thanks for the... Well thanks for nothing," I said as I began to float on.

The zombie pigmen looked at me, shook their fists, and called me a fool. "You will regret that insult," one of them shouted.

I ignored him. *What is so foolish about wanting to explore your world?*

As I floated away, I heard one of the pigmen ask another, "Hey, did you rip one? It smells like a fart."

The Nether must have strange gases emerging from the ground. Everyone I meet seems to smell farts. The weird thing is, I didn't.

Chapter 4

I floated through a couple more chambers in my new home of the Nether.

I saw several small lava flows which gave off a warm orange glow. I spent some time floating in the heat rising from the lava. It felt good as it warmed my tentacles.

The warmth of the lava made me feel tired. I could feel

myself drifting to sleep. My high-pitched cat noises became very, very quiet as I drifted into sleep.

I was not sure how long I had been asleep when something bumped into me, waking me up. When I came to my senses, I saw that it was another ghast!

"You awake yet sleepy head?" asked the ghast.

"Yeah, bro. Stop bumping me," I said rubbing my sleepy eyes with my tentacles.

"Chill, bro," said the ghast. "I saw you floating there like a dead creature and wanted to wake you up so we could talk. My name is Jake."

I smiled.

Or, at least, I felt like I was smiling. But, I'm not sure if I can smile because my mouth always seems to be shaped like a flat line. Maybe that's just how we ghasts look.

"My name is Todd," I said excitedly, my chill exterior momentarily disappearing. "I just spawned today."

Jake laughed. "Well, I'll have to show you around," he

said. "I spawned about a week ago, so I know what's up."

"Awesome," I said. "What should we do first?"

"Well, why don't I take you to meet all of my friends, and after that, we can decide on something to do as a group?" suggested Jake.

"That sounds cool," I said. "I've been floating around for a while looking for some more ghasts like me to hang out with."

"Great," said Jake. "Follow me."

"Cool," I said.

Then, Jake stopped for a moment and asked, "Say, uh, did you just fart or something?"

"No," I said. "Why?"

"It smells farty all of a sudden," Jake said. "Weird. Anyway, let's go."

Chapter 5

Jake took me to meet two of his friends: Ralph and Cindy. We introduced ourselves and then I asked, "So, what do you guys to do all day?"

"Well, we like to float around and makc cat noises and explore the Nether," said Cindy.

"Yeah, the Nether's full of all sorts of strange things," said Ralph.

"What do you mean strange things? Are they dangerous?" I asked, my tentacles quivering with fear.

Jake moved his tentacles back and forth to calm me down and said, "No, nothing is really dangerous in the Nether." Then he paused for a moment and added, "Except Herobrine."

"Herobrine? Who is Herobrine?" I asked.

All of the three other ghasts looked at each other. They seemed surprised that I had not heard of Herobrine. They also looked frightened.

"Herobrine is a mysterious figure who spends most of his time in the Nether. He looks a lot like a player, but he has glowing white eyes and the ability to do just about anything," said Cindy.

"Yeah, Herobrine is super dominant and kind of a jerk," said Ralph. "He likes to destroy things others have created, and he enjoys killing."

"You see, Todd," said Jake. "Herobrine is just a strange evil guy who you want to avoid. If you see him ... well ... it's probably too late."

I did not like thinking about some mysterious evil dude who might sneak up on me and do bad things to me. It just wasn't right. It totally destroyed my normal ghast chill.

"I guess we should stick together then for protection," I said.

The other three ghasts agreed and we resumed our floating exploration of the Nether.

But, before we did, Cindy said, "Hey, does anyone else smell that? It smells like a fart."

"Not me," said Ralph.

"Not me," said Jake.

"Not me," I said.

"Weird," said Cindy. "I could have sworn I smelled a fart."

Chapter 6

We floated through a few chambers and saw nothing other than some lava flows here and there, dripping from the ceiling into pools below.

The other ghasts warned me about drops of lava from the ceiling and that they could seriously harm me or maybe even kill me.

This seemed to be the only random danger in the Nether. The other ghasts told me that ghasts were considered to be passive mobs. This meant that everyone ignored them and they went about their business without any problem.

"The only things you have to worry about are players who want to harvest your tears for potions," said Jake. "If a ghast sees a player, it becomes hostile in order to defend itself."

I started to shiver. My tentacles were vibrating with fear and anxiety.

"Really?" I said in disbelief. "So, we just float around doing nothing, meowing like cats until someone comes and kills us?"

"Gee, Todd, don't make our lives sound so lame and pointless," said Ralph.

"Oh, I didn't mean that our ... our lives were ... pointless," I stammered. "But, it does seem kind of stupid that we actually do nothing and are passive all the time until we encounter a player."

"You have to look on the bright side, Todd," said Jake. "We get to float around the Nether and see all kinds of amazing things with our lives. There are a lot of creatures in the world who never get to see anything amazing. They just live in some deep, dark hideous place where nothing ever happens and nothing else lives."

"Check out the big brain on Jake," said Cindy.

"Oh, be quiet Cindy," said Jake.

"I guess it can be nice to spend your whole life looking at interesting things," I said. "I'll try it for a while."

"Great," said Jake. He paused for a moment and sniffed the air. "Dang, there is that fart smell again. Sure it wasn't one of you?"

We all shook our head and then resumed our pointless floating through Nether.

Chapter 7

We had been floating around looking at various things. Jake, Ralph and Cindy introduced me to some more magma cubes and zombie pigmen.

I liked meeting new mobs, but there didn't seem to be any other varieties in the Nether.

We probably had been floating for only about two or

three hours, and I was already getting bored. I shouldn't have been.

Just then, a player walked into the chamber. The other three ghasts started to yell very loudly and then rushed toward the player, shooting fireballs at him.

The player began shooting arrows towards Jake, Ralph and Cindy. One arrow hit Cindy and she had to back away from the fight for a moment.

"Come on Todd," yelled Jake. "Help us kill this guy!"

"But okay, but how? What we do?" I asked in panic.

"What are you a noob?" said Ralph. "Shoot fireballs out of your mouth!"

Once he said it, it was so obvious. What a fool I was. Of course I shoot fire out of my mouth. I'm a ghast.

I swished my tentacles and zoomed toward the player. I screeched as loudly as I could, sounding like a ferocious kitty cat, and then I blasted him with... a ... giant ... cloud of ... fart gas?

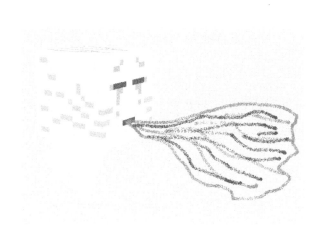

The other ghasts stopped
blowing fireballs and looked at
me with expressions of horror
on their faces.

"It was you," said Cindy in
shock. "You were the reason
we kept smelling farts!"

The player put his bow
down to his side and stared at
the giant hideous dark cloud

oozing towards him. He looked at it quizzically, as if he had never seen anything like it.

When the cloud reached him he doubled over and was retching on the ground. He continued retching as he tried to crawl out of the radius of the fart cloud, but he could not do it.

Soon, he was dead from a fart overdose, and he evaporated into a puff of smoke, dropping his inventory.

Chapter 8

Cindy, Ralph, and Jake stared at me and at the now dissipating fart cloud.

I looked back at them and said, "What? I tried to make a fireball and that's what came out."

"Dude, that was the most disgusting thing I've ever seen or smelled," said Ralph.

"Yeah, Todd, that *was* pretty rank," added Cindy.

"Correction," said Jake, "that was the single most hideous and disgusting and horrible and gross and nasty thing that has ever been seen by anyone who's ever lived in the Nether."

I felt horrible. I wondered why it had happened.

"So none of the other ghasts have fart breath?" I asked, feeling ashamed.

All of the ghasts shook their tentacles to indicate there was no such thing. "No, Todd, you are the only ghast I've ever met with fart breath," said Jake.

"In fact, you are the only *creature* I've ever even heard of to have fart breath," said Cindy. "Not even Herobrine has fart breath."

"Well, guys, I will understand if you don't want to be my friends anymore," I said sadly. "I know how hideous and disgusting it must be to look at me and think about the diabolical fart stench that will come out of my mouth if I ever have to defend myself."

"Dude, don't get so melodramatic on us," said Cindy. "It was pretty awesome how your fart cloud suffocated that player to death with its hideousness."

"Yeah," said Jake. "I mean, it was the most hideous thing I've ever smelled in my life and I almost think it would be better to be dead than to continue living with the memory of that smell, but … it is a pretty awesome weapon."

I smiled because these other ghasts were not going to abandon me just because I was a little different – okay, I was a *lot* different – but they still wanted to be my friends.

"Okay, guys," I said. "What should we do now?"

"Well, I think maybe we should just go to sleep for a while," said Cindy. "Usually once you kill a player, you don't see another player for weeks. For some reason, it takes a long time for them to find this part of the Nether."

"Okay, I am pretty tired after that battle," I said.

"Yeah, and I'm pretty tired after smelling your hideous

breath," said Ralph with a chuckle.

And so, we all decided to fall asleep floating in that very spot where we learned that my breath was fart breath.

Chapter 9

The next few days were uneventful. No players showed up and there was no need for any of us to use our fire (or fart) breath for defense.

However, one morning, our calm repose was shattered.

We were floating along when we heard a rumbling coming from up ahead.

"I wonder what it could be?" said Ralph.

We did not have to wait long to learn was making the noise. It was a large group of zombie pigmen fleeing from something. They entered the chamber in which we were floating at a high rate of speed.

"Get out of the way," moaned one of the pigmen.

"What are you cowards running from?" asked Jake.

"Just run," said another pigman.

"Float away from here you stupid ghasts," said a third pigman.

I wondered what could cause so many zombie pigmen to run away. If it were a player, that many pigmen could have easily killed him, though some of them surely would have died as well.

Maybe there was a disaster with a lava flow or something, I thought.

"Come on, won't one of you undead weirdoes tell us what is going on?" shouted Cindy.

Finally, one of the zombie pigmen stopped and looked at all of us. His face was serious and stern. He said, "Herobrine comes."

"Oh, no," I said.

"And, Herobrine said he was searching for ghast tears," said the pigman.

"What do you mean?" I asked, totally freaking out.

"Herobrine is worse than any player. Worse than one hundred players," said Cindy. "He slaughters ghasts and harvests our tears by the gallon."

My tentacles began to shake with fear. I wondered what we should do.

"I guess we better get out of here, guys," said Jake.

"I've never seen Herobrine," said Ralph. "I think we should hang out and get a look at him."

"That's crazy," said Cindy. "If Herobrine sees you, you will be dead right away. Just one look from him is enough to kill you."

"Oh that's a bunch of nonsense," said Ralph. "No one

can kill you just been looking at you."

"Well, I heard Herobrine could," said Jake.

I looked at my three friends. I did not want to see any of them die. But, I had to admit I was curious about this Herobrine monster. I wondered what could possibly cause all those zombie pigmen run away.

What did Herobrine really look like? Did he really have glowing white eyes like everyone said? Was he really as powerful and evil as my friends said?

"I'm with Ralph," I said, almost not believing the words were coming out of my mouth. "I think we should hide and see what Herobrine is really like."

"I know I'm going to regret this, but I'll stay too," said Cindy with a heavy sigh.

Jake raised one of his tentacles and pointed up toward a corner of the room. "It looks like there's a little alcove up there where we can hide.

I'm sure Herobrine won't be looking up there for us."

It seemed like a good idea to the rest of us, so we floated up to the little hidden alcove near the ceiling of the chamber to await the arrival of Herobrine.

Chapter 10

We got into position just as the last of the zombie pigmen left the large chamber in which we were located.

We huddled together so that we could hide in the small alcove Jake had noticed. The height of the alcove wall was just enough that we could peek our heads over and stare down to the floor of the chamber many blocks below without being seen.

"This is a really good spot," whispered Ralph. "We will be able to see Herobrine when he walks through the entrance to the chamber."

"Yeah, it is perfect," said Cindy.

"I can't believe we are doing this," I said. "All the other ghasts will be jealous when we tell them about it."

"Be quiet you guys, we can't tell anyone about Herobrine if he hears us and destroys us," said Jake.

When he said that, I got really freaked out. I realized that this was a life-and-death situation. This was serious and insane. I was regretting my decision to stay here. But it was too late now.

No one spoke after that. We waited quietly for what seemed like hours but it was only a few minutes.

Then, we saw him.

Herobrine walked into the chamber without any attempt to hide. It was as if he viewed the Nether as his kingdom.

We watched in awe as Herobrine looked toward a lava flow and lava rose out of the ground and formed itself into a bottle of obsidian. Then more lava went inside the bottle of obsidian and finally it formed an obsidian stopper to close the bottle. The bottle then floated towards Herobrine's outstretched hand, and he grabbed it and tucked it into his inventory.

"Oh my gosh," whispered Cindy "that was insane."

"Shut up," whispered Jake.

We then watched as Herobrine turned and looked back from where he'd come. He motioned his arm as if beckoning something.

We all looked toward the entrance to the chamber waiting for something horrible, hideous and disturbing to enter the room. We waited and waited and waited. Herobrine stood there also waiting.

Finally, a killer bunny hopped into the chamber.

Chapter 11

The killer bunny sat obediently at Herobrine's feet. Herobrine reached down and stroked its ears.

I watched as Herobrine seemed to show love and affection for the killer bunny.

Maybe Herobrine was not as evil as my friends had said?

Herobrine reached into his pocket and pulled out a large

carrot. He held it above the bunny and said, "Do you want this yummy carrot, Mr. Soft Ears?"

Mr. Soft Ears nodded his head up and down. He jumped up and down a couple of times to show his enthusiastic desire to eat the carrot.

"Well, then, Mr. Soft Ears, you need to earn it," said Herobrine.

The killer bunny became more excited and agitated. He jumped up and down in a frenzy.

Boy, did he really want that carrot!

"Do you know what you can do to earn the carrot?" asked Herobrine.

The bunny suddenly became still and sat very quietly, listening for his task.

"You can," began Herobrine, as he turned and looked directly at our hiding place and extended a finger pointing at our location, "kill those ghasts!"

Oh, no!

The killer bunny darted towards us.

Cindy screamed.

Ralph peed his tentacles.

Jake tried to shoot some fireballs, but he was so scared, he could not make even a spark.

I floated up. I had to do something. I took a deep breath and then exhaled.

A dark, dank, thick cloud oozed from my mouth. Even I could smell how hideous and disgusting it was.

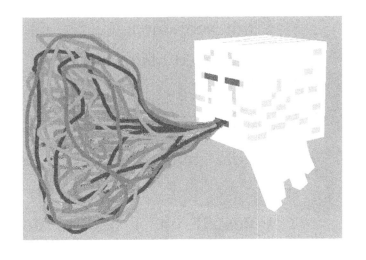

The bunny momentarily halted his charge, staring at the strange cloud. Then, the bunny shrugged and continued his attack.

But, the bunny did not get far. He slammed into the edge of the fart cloud, took one breath, and died instantly.

"Nooooo!" screamed Herobrine. "Not Mr. Soft Ears! You will pay for this."

Herobrine pulled out the lava-filled obsidian bottle and tossed it at us. As the bottle came toward us, the lid opened, and the hot lava began to spill out.

At the same time, my fart cloud was edging ever closer to Herobrine.

Would it be able to harm him? Maybe even kill him?

When the hot lava came into contact with the hideous

fart gas, something I was not expecting happened.

It exploded!

My friends and I were slammed against the wall by the force of the explosion. I saw stars from hitting my head. I could not tell which way was up for a few moments.

But, soon, I regained my sense of direction and floated up to see what had become of IIcrobrine.

Where he had been standing was a giant pit. A deep abyss of doom.

"Guys," I said. "Guys, I think Herobrine is dead."

"I doubt it," said Ralph.

"I agree with Ralph," said Cindy. "Herobrine might have been defeated today, but he is not dead."

"Besides," said Jake, "Even if you did kill him, he would just respawn. He is immortal."

"Do you think he will try to get revenge on us?" I said, my tentacles shaking with worry.

"Probably," said Jake. "That is why we have to keep you around. You and your nasty fart breath are our secret weapon."

"Plus, the Nether is a big place," said Cindy. "Even Herobrine can't be everywhere at once. Can he?"

The End

Also by M.T. Lott:

Diary of a Farting Villager

Annabelle, the Reluctant Fart Fairy

The Farting Animals Coloring Book

Printed in Great Britain
by Amazon

81801637R00048